The Princess,
the Mud Pies,
and the Dragon

adapted by Lily Ernesto
illustrated by Oki Han

HOUGHTON MIFFLIN COMPANY

BOSTON

ATLANTA   DALLAS   GENEVA, ILLINOIS   PALO ALTO   PRINCETON

In a land far away, a sweet princess lived
in a castle with her mother the queen
and her father the king.

The princess had toys of gold and toys of silver.
But she never played with them.
All day long, the princess made mud pies.

The king and queen said,
"You have toys of gold and toys of silver.
Why do you play with mud pies?"

"I just like mud pies," said the princess,
and she made some more. At the end of the day,
she left her pies in a wagon to dry.

Now in this land, there lived a dragon.
That dragon loved toys of gold and
toys of silver, and he wanted more.

Late one night, the dragon came to the castle,
but he did not get very far.
He banged his foot on the princess's wagon.

Ooooo!
This made the dragon very mad!
Fire shot from his mouth.

The next morning, the princess went out to play.
"Oh look!" she cried. "The dragon has been here.
He has melted all my toys of gold
and all my toys of silver."

Then the princess began to smile.
"Look," she cried again. "The dragon has
cooked my mud pies. See! They are all hard."

The princess took the pies to her room
and put them by the window to cool.

Late at night, the dragon came back to the castle.
This time he got as far as the princess's window.
Crash! Clatter! Tinkle!
He knocked the mud pies to the floor!

What a noise!
It scared the dragon so much he started to run.
He ran until he was so far away, no one
ever saw him again.

The king and queen hugged the princess.
"Your mud pies saved us all!" they said.

Now the princess still makes mud pies.
And so do the king, the queen, and all
the king's soldiers. They cook them in the oven.

Then they put the pies by all the windows to cool—
and just in case another dragon comes to
the castle late at night.